PANTHER DREAM

To the children, to
All of life, to all that is,
Now and forever.

Text Copyright © 1991 by Robert Weir and Wendy Weir
Illustrations Copyright © 1991 Wendy Weir
All rights reserved.
Printed in the United States of America
FIRST EDITION
10 9 8 7 6 5 4 3 2 1

Library of Congress Cataloging-in-Publication Data
Weir, Bob, 1947-
Panther dream : a story of the African rainforest / Bob and Wendy
Weir ; illustrated by Wendy Weir.
p.   cm.
Summary: While hunting for food in the rain forest for his
starving village, a young boy encounters a panther that teaches him
how to conserve life in the rain forest.
ISBN 1-56282-075-3 (lib. bdg.)   Book-and-cassette package: 1-56282-076-1
[1. Rain forests—Fiction.   2. Jungle animals—Fiction.
3. Wildlife conservation—Fiction.   4. Africa—Fiction.]
I. Weir, Wendy, 1949-   ill.   II. Title
PZ7.W4369Pan 1991   [E]—dc20   91-71385   CIP   AC

The artwork for each picture consists of
acrylic paints mixed with water
on Strathmore Bristol Board.

For more information about the African
rainforest, contact:

Mr. Simon Muchiru
Executive Director
African NGO's Environment Network
P.O. Box 53844
Nairobi, Kenya

Mr. Randy Hayes
Executive Director
Rainforest Action Network
301 Broadway
San Francisco, CA 94133

The Walt Disney Company has arranged
to have a tree planted for every
tree used in printing this book.

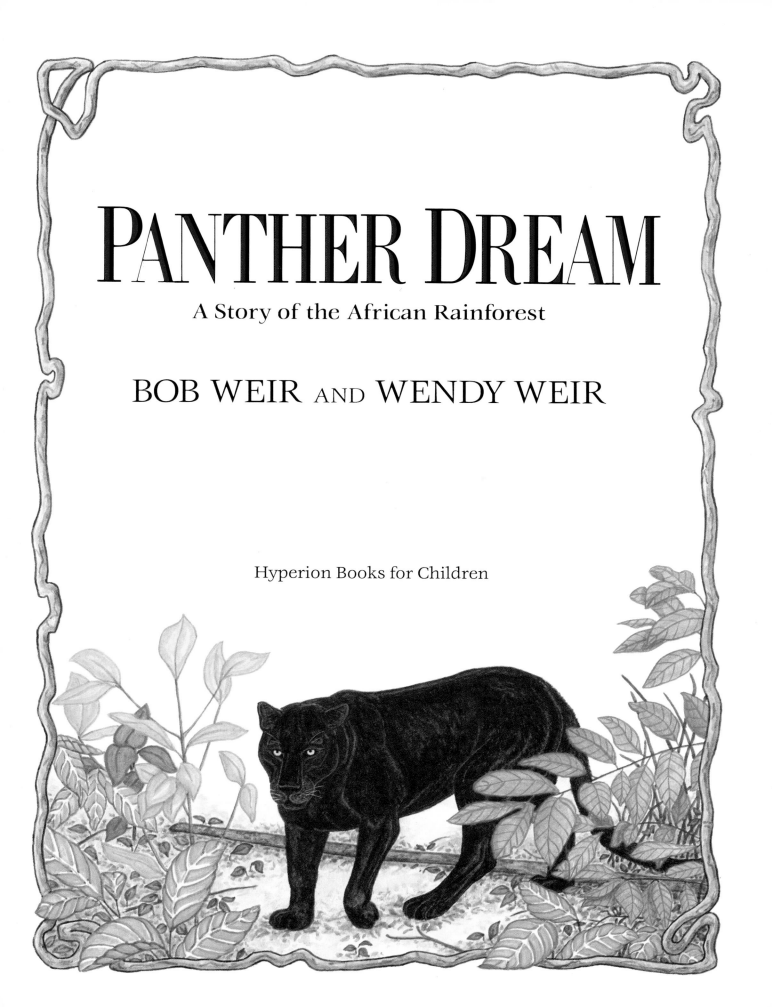

PANTHER DREAM

A Story of the African Rainforest

BOB WEIR AND WENDY WEIR

Hyperion Books for Children

It is midafternoon in the African rainforest. There is no breeze. The air is hot and humid. The mass of shaded green is broken only by shafts

of light filtering down through the trees to the forest floor. The whir of cicadas and the buzz and scrape of insects penetrate the stillness.

In the middle of the rainforest is a small farming village where Lokuli, a young boy, and his family live. He is not allowed to enter the rainforest because the villagers believe it is full of evil spirits. The are content to trade their crops of bananas, peanuts, and corn with the forest-dwelling Pygmies for wild meat and honey.

Today, Lokuli is worried. He had heard his father talking to another man from his village, "Soon we will need more meat for our families. The Pygmies have no meat to trade. They say the 'keti,' the forest spirits, have hunted it first. What will we do?"

Lokuli goes in search of his grandmother. Many years ago, she left her Pygmy home in the forest to live with his grandfather in the farming village, but she has never forgotten the ways of the rainforest. Often, she tells him wonderful stories about her childhood. How can there be evil spirits in the rainforest, Lokuli wonders, if my grandmother lived there?

Lokuli finds his grandmother grinding corn behind their mud hut. He squats next to her. "Grandmother, tell me what it was like to go hunting when you were a young girl."

"Dear Lokuli," she replies, "I have told you that story many times. Why do you want to hear it now?"

"It is my favorite. Please, grandmother!"

She looks at him curiously, and begins. "When I was young, Lokuli, whenever we needed meat, the whole tribe would go on a hunt. We would track the duiker and small antelope deep into the forest. Sometimes when we got close, we would find one of their carcasses high in the tree branches.

"When I was little, my father would laugh and tell me it had flown there like a bird. But as I got older, I learned that a panther or leopard had killed the animal and stored it there to eat.

"When we arrived at a good spot, some of my tribe would stretch a big net across the forest floor between the trees and bushes. Others would take spears and walk farther into the forest. After a while, they would turn around and come back toward the net making lots of noise. The small antelope and duiker would be scared by the noise and run away from the hunters. As they ran into the net and became trapped, the hunters would kill them with their spears and prepare the meat to take home. Then the whole tribe would rejoice and thank the forest for her gifts. My father was a great hunter. I keep his spear in our hut."

"Grandmother," Lokuli exclaims, "I am going to go hunting just like you! Father says that our village needs meat, but he and the other

farmers are afraid of the forest. I am not afraid! Can I use your spear?"

"I am glad you are so brave, my child," she replies. "But you do not know how to hunt and your father has forbidden you to enter the forest. He will be very angry with you."

Lokuli knows this is true, but he hopes if he finds meat, his father will understand. As he gets up to leave, he looks down at his grandmother. She says nothing, but the sparkle in her eyes reassures him.

Lokuli walks quickly into his house. It is empty because his mother works all day in the cornfields with the other women. He slips on his T-shirt, grabs the spear, and runs swiftly out the door to the Pygmy trail at the edge of the forest. Once on the trail, he knows no one will follow.

   As Lokuli goes deeper into the rainforest, he is startled by the screeching of a family of black-and-white colobus monkeys high above. He looks up. In the canopy of trees, over one hundred feet above the ground, they leap from branch to branch using their white plumed tails for balance.

Undisturbed by their movement, an African long-tailed hawk swoops down in search of small birds and animals to eat. Sensing danger, a giant forest squirrel runs for cover while two talkative gray parrots become quiet until the hawk passes.

Down in the understory, Lokuli sees a big black-and-white casqued hornbill perching on a tree limb, calling loudly to his mate nesting inside a hole in the trunk. Awakened by the noise, a scaly-tailed flying squirrel leaps from a branch to glide more than fifty feet through the air to another tree.

Lokuli turns his attention back to the trail. Passing beneath a fallen tree, he does not notice a large black form stretched out above him. Aware of a strange scent, the panther slowly opens his eyes. He is full from eating but is curious about the smell and looks down.

Lokuli walks on, unaware that he is being observed by a pair of bright yellow eyes. Suddenly, he hears a loud noise. He knows it must be close because sound doesn't travel far in the jungle. He tries to find its direction, but the noise bounces off the trees making it impossible to locate.

It must be a huge animal, Lokuli thinks, pushing its way through the forest. But what is it? Where is it? Clutching his spear tightly, he looks carefully around trying to catch some movement. The noise gets louder and louder, closer and closer.

A tree branch breaks to his left. The loud crack startles Lokuli. Turning quickly, he sees a large elephant lumber into sight.

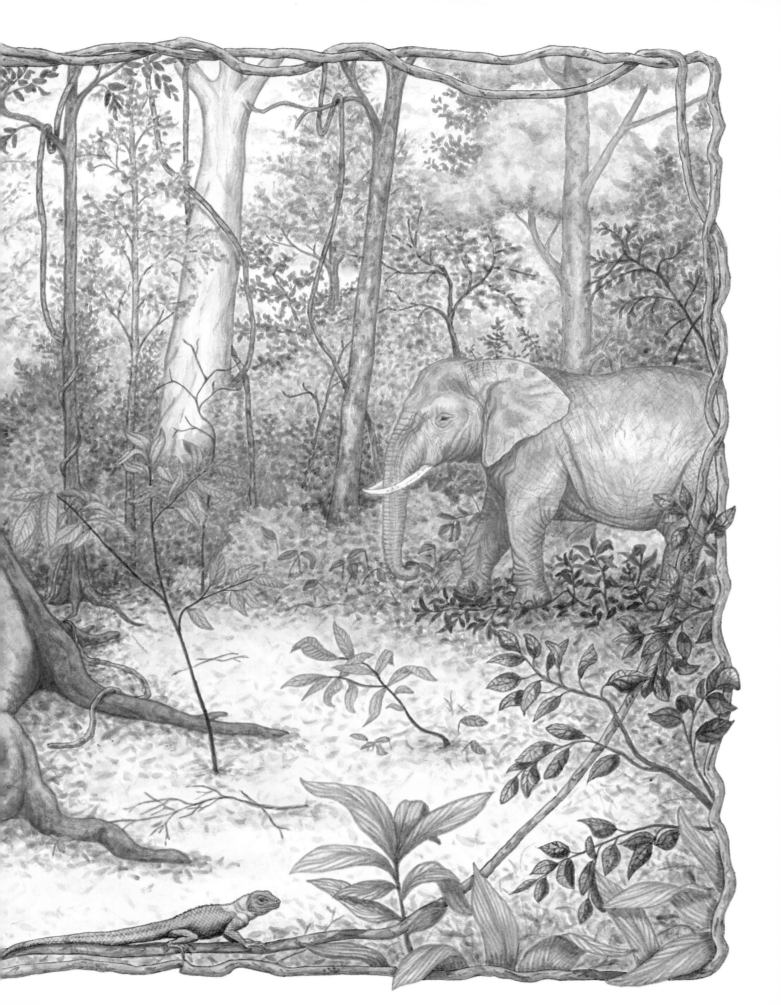

Lokuli runs behind the wide buttress of a tree for protection. The elephant sees the movement and stops, then turns in his direction. After long minutes of quiet, the elephant loses interest and continues on his journey.

Lokuli breathes a sigh of relief, then returns to the hunt. Under a strangling fig tree, he finds small hoofprints in the mud. "The duiker must be near!" he whispers. With increasing excitement, he leaves the path to follow the tracks. Unobserved, two bright yellow eyes watch him pass.

The tracks cross larger hoofprints, then disappear into a clearing. Discouraged, Lokuli walks over to an old moss-covered tree, lays his spear against its fallen trunk, and sits down to think. Fast-moving rain clouds hide the sun and the softness of a rising breeze lulls Lokuli to sleep. In the stillness, a shy okapi wanders by eating leaves from the low branches.

Lokuli is awakened by the loud cries of chimpanzees above, but the rest of the forest seems at peace. The sound of cicadas and insects surround him.

A sunbird darts through the air on its way to flowers high in the canopy. Two large drops of water glisten in a bush. Yet Lokuli feels uneasy.

Looking around once again, Lokuli stops and stares. The drops of water move and blink. Blink?

The branches in front of him rustle, then slowly part as a large black panther creeps cautiously into the clearing. Lokuli is so scared he cannot move. They stare at each other in silence.

"Why are you in our rainforest?" Lokuli feels the panther say.

"I am hunting game for my village," Lokuli replies in his thoughts. "They need meat."

"I see that you are young and do not know the ways of the forest," the panther responds. "Respect all life within it. If you need meat, take only enough to live on. Then life here can continue."

Without warning, a crack of lightning and boom of thunder rip through the warm, humid air. In the distance, a large tree crashes to the ground. For a second, Lokuli looks up at the sky. When he looks back, the panther is gone. Maybe it was only a dream, he wonders.

The storm soon passes. Lokuli looks at the sun and sees that it is getting late. He is hungry and thirsty, but he must find meat for his village before he returns home. He decides to go back to the Pygmy trail and hunt for game along the way.

At the edge of the clearing, he stops to cut a hanging liana with his spear and drinks the water stored inside. Then he enters the jungle to find the path, but he cannot see it because of the dense bushes. Knowing the trail is not far away, he continues on.

Gradually, the sounds of the forest change. The buzz of katydids and croak of frogs begin. Mosquitos come out and seek the warmth of his body. A fruit bat flies past. The forest darkens. Still Lokuli cannot find the path. He looks around, becoming more and more scared. He is lost.

In the fading light, he enters a clearing. In the center, a bright glow shines from a newly fallen tree. He walks over and finds that the tree had been struck by lightning during the storm. By adding twigs and leaves to the glowing embers he is able to make a small fire for protection from the dark.

As Lokuli sits quietly next to the fire, he notices the night animals coming out one by one. A little dormouse climbs the trunk in search of food.

It stops to sniff curiously at a snail before scampering off.

From the flickering shadows, a bush baby leaps to a nearby branch looking for insects. It briefly stares at the fire, then moves swiftly away.

A civet stalks around the circle of light, investigating the strange human scent, but the fire scares him and he too disappears into the darkness.

Soon Lokuli's fear is overcome by exhaustion. He lies down on the tree trunk and falls fast asleep, unaware of a giant pangolin sniffing for termites in the bark near his feet.

At dawn, the sounds of the night are replaced by a loud chorus of cicadas, birds, and monkeys calling through the jungle. Lokuli sits up, letting the rising sun warm his body. Looking around, his eyes suddenly stop. Across the clearing next to a tree is a Pygmy staring at him!

Lokuli stands up and stares back at the man who looks so much like his grandmother. "You must be from the farming village nearby," the

man says. "Do not be afraid. I am Abusa and I trade with them. Why are you here?"

"I came to hunt meat for my village, but I couldn't find any. When I turned to go home last night, I became lost. Do you have any meat? We need it very badly," Lokuli explains.

"I am sorry, we have no meat," Abusa replies. "We are here to gather honey. Come help us. When we are done, I will take you home."

All morning, Lokuli works happily with the honey gatherers. As pieces of honeycomb drop from the tree, he picks them up and fills his mouth before filling the basket. His empty stomach soon becomes full with rich, sweet honey. When they are finished, Abusa fills a small basket with honey and looks at Lokuli. "Let us leave now. The trip will not take long."

As they walk back through the forest, Abusa teaches Lokuli how to hunt. "Look here." Abusa stops and points to the ground. "There has been a fresh kill. The pawprints on the ground show it was done by a large panther. It might still be near. We must be careful."

The panther! It wasn't a dream! Lokuli thinks. As he looks around, his eyes are drawn to a small tree. In the shadows are two bright yellow eyes. Lokuli gasps. The he senses the panther say, "I have brought you food for your family. It is a gift of the forest. Look up and you will have meat."

Lokuli does not believe this, but he looks up and in the branches above his head is the carcass of a duiker. He lets out a yell. "Abusa, we have meat! Look!" Abusa looks up and smiles. "If you wish to take the duiker home, we must hurry before the panther returns."

While Abusa prepares the meat, Lokuli looks around to say good-bye to the panther, but he does not see it. So with his heart he sends his thanks to the panther and the forest, then follows Abusa home.

When they walk into the farming village, Lokuli's family rushes out to meet them. "Where have you been?" his father asks angrily. But when he sees the meat and honey they have brought, he rejoices. "You have saved our village from hunger, my son. We are very grateful."

"I did not do this," Lokuli explains. "These are gifts from the rain-forest. The forest is not full of evil spirits as you say. It is our friend."

That evening, while the meat is roasting over the fire, Lokuli tells his story to the villagers. But he does not mention the black panther. He still does not know if it was real or only a dream. From the darkness beyond the fire, two bright yellow eyes blink, then disappear.

TROPICAL RAINFORESTS

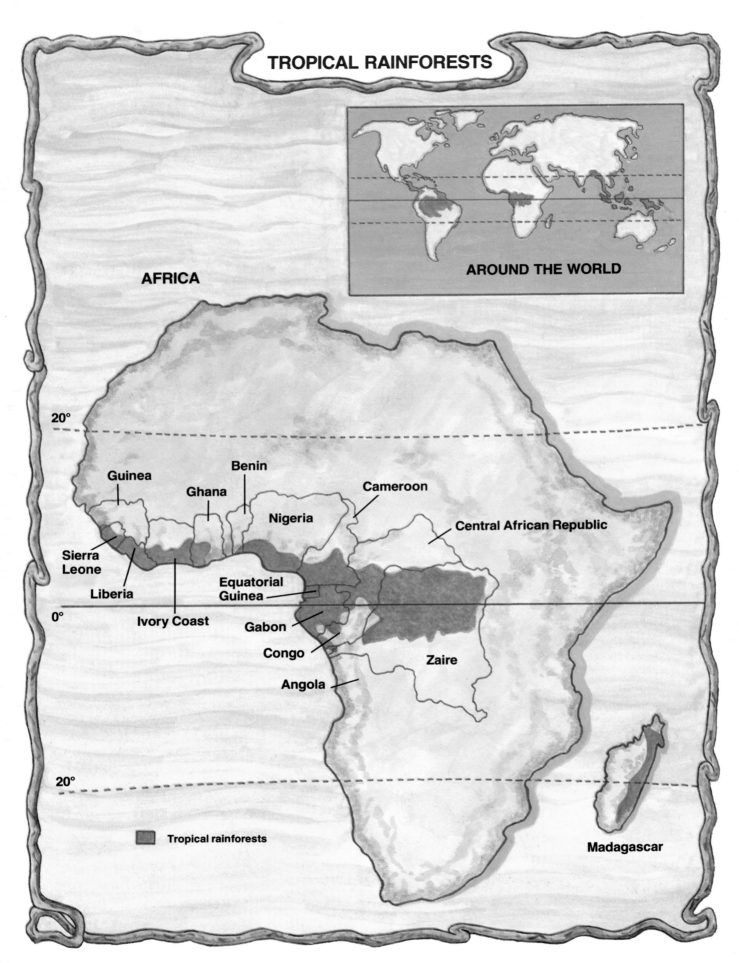

AROUND THE WORLD

AFRICA

20°

Guinea

Benin

Ghana

Cameroon

Nigeria

Central African Republic

Sierra
Leone

Liberia

Equatorial
Guinea

0°

Ivory Coast

Gabon

Congo

Zaire

Angola

20°

Tropical rainforests

Madagascar

Key to the Illustrations

Animal and Plant Names

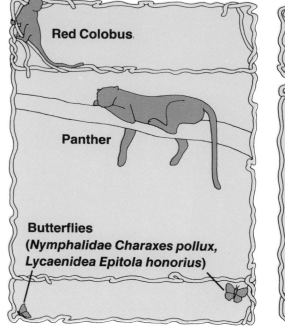

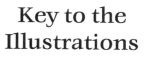

Front Cover—Red Colobus, Panther, Butterflies (*Nymphalidae Charaxes pollux, Lycaenidea Epitola honorius*)

Copyright Page— Sunbird, Mandrill

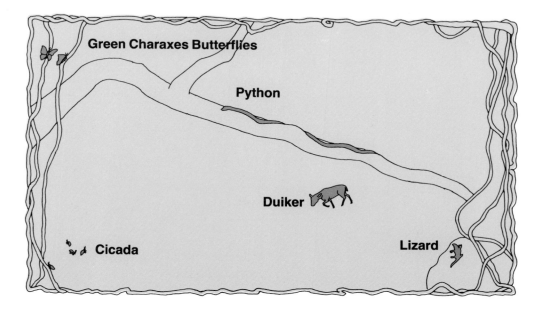

Pages 4 & 5—Green Charaxes Butterflies, Python, Duiker, Cicada, Lizard

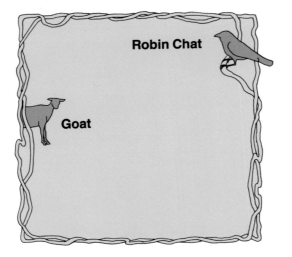

Page 7 — Goat, Robin Chat

Page 8 — Bush Squirrels

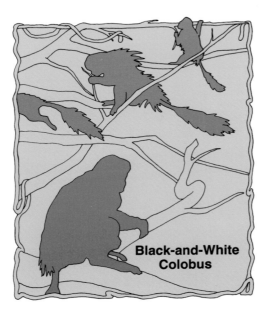

Page 12 — Black-and-White Colobus

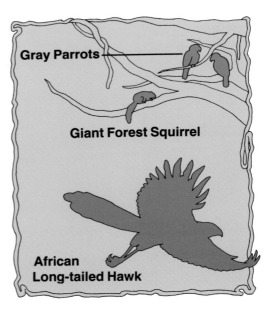

Page 13 — Gray Parrots,
Giant Forest Squirrel,
African Long-tailed Hawk

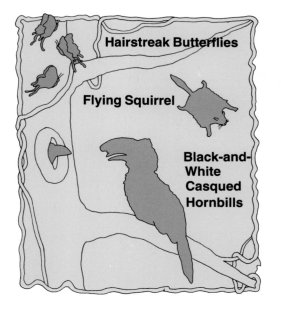

Page 14—Hairstreak Butterflies,
Flying Squirrel,
Black-and-White Casqued Hornbills

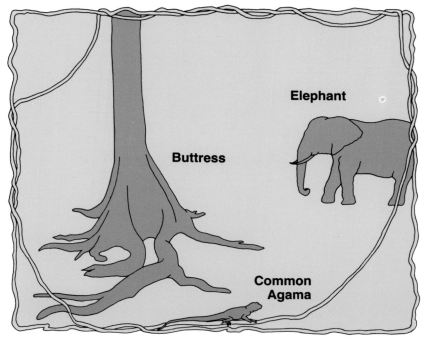

Pages 16 & 17—Elephant, Buttress,
Common Agama

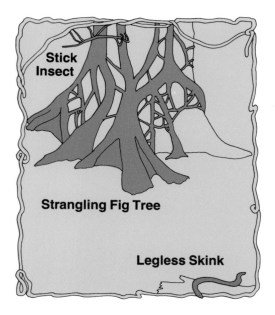

Page 19—Stick Insect,
Strangling Fig Tree,
Legless Skink

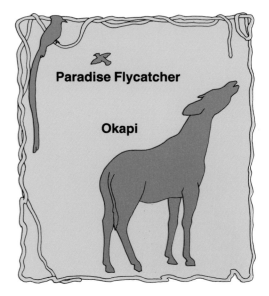

Page 20—Okapi,
Paradise Flycatcher

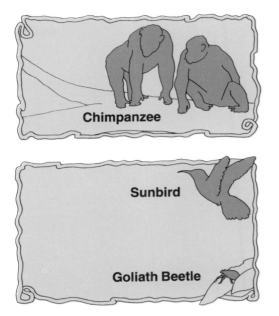

Page 21 — Chimpanzee, Sunbird, Goliath Beetle

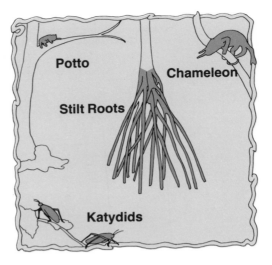

Page 24 — Potto, Stilt Roots, Chameleon, Katydids

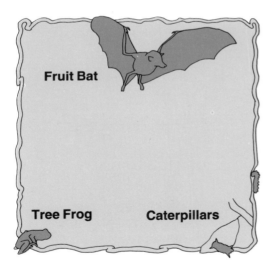

Page 25 — Fruit Bat, Tree Frog, Caterpillars

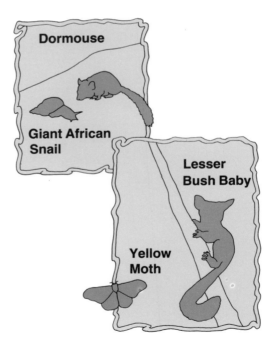

Page 26 — Giant African Snail, Dormouse, Yellow Moth, Lesser Bush Baby

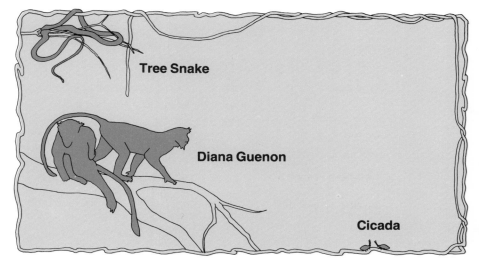

Page 27 — African Civet,
Giant Pangolin

Pages 28-29 — Tree Snake, Diana Guenon,
Cicada

Page 30 — Golden Sparrow

Back Cover — Black-masked Lovebirds, Bees

GLOSSARY

Antelope	A swift, deerlike animal.
Buttress	Wings spreading out from the base of a tree trunk; they keep the tree upright against the force of wind. Some buttresses reach fifteen feet high.
Carcass	The dead body of an animal.
Casqued Hornbill	A large bird with a huge, curved bill.
Cicada	A sapsucking insect which flies in the canopy during the daytime.
Civet	A catlike animal with spotted fur.
Duiker	A small deerlike animal, weighing up to forty pounds.
Katydid	A flying green-tree insect that comes out in the evening.
Liana	A woody, thick vine that hangs from trees.
Okapi	An African animal related to the giraffe.
Pangolin	A toothless, scaly animal that rolls into a ball when attacked.
Panther	*Panthera pardus.* A black leopard found throughout the rainforests of Africa and Asia.
Pygmy	A race of small people, less than five feet in height, who have lived in tribes scattered across equatorial Africa for many thousands of years.
Spirit	An unseen being or energy force, not of this world.
Rainforest	In this context, rainforest refers to an equatorial evergreen forest with high rainfall (160″ to 400″ per year), a high average temperature (80°F), and no pronounced cold or dry spells. The levels of a rainforest are
Canopy	The tops or crowns of the middle level of trees, ranging from 100′ to 130′ high.
Understory	The level under the canopy consisting of shrubs, non-woody plants, seedlings and young trees.
Floor	The ground level, often bare except for a thin layer of dead leaves and an occasional fallen tree.

The African rainforest supports approximately 335,000 plant and animal species. It is conservatively estimated that rainforests overall support two million species or two-fifths of all those on Earth.